ALBERT'S
ALMOST
AMAZING ADVENTURE

Sean & Owen —

Be Amazing!

Marty Kelley

WRITTEN AND ILLUSTRATED BY
MARTY KELLEY

ISLANDPORT PRESS

Text © 2016 by Marty Kelley
Illustrations © 2016 by Marty Kelley

Published by Islandport Press
P.O. Box 10
Yarmouth, Maine 04096
books@islandportpress.com
www.islandportpress.com

ISBN: 978-1-939017-69-7
Library of Congress Control Number: 2015945262
Production Date: November 2015
Plant & Location: Printed by We SP Corporation (Gyunggi-do, Korea)
Job / Batch #: 55802-0

PLAYGROUND

Dedicated to the amazing people
at the Margret and H.A. Rey Center
in Waterville Valley, NH.
Thank you all for helping me
to make this book happen!

Hey! Albert's back from his trip to Maine!

Hi, Albert.

Hi, guys. My trip was amazing! I made a new friend
and we did all kinds of AMAZING things!

We went to lots of amazing places and saw some amazing things.

We went to the beach one day.

While we were there, I saw a man eating—

SHARK?!?

A giant, man-eating great white shark that was looking
for a kid to eat?
But you jumped on its back and rode it away
and saved the day?

Umm. . . no. No.
Actually, it was a man eating
a big hot dog.
Some mustard dribbled off it, but none
of it landed on his shirt!

That was SO amazing!

But not as amazing as when we went
to my grandmother's house.

We walked in the front door and discovered that my grandmother had become a—

And she tried to feed you to her zombie cats?
But you defeated her with your secret
ninja kung-fu powers?

Umm . . . no. No.
Actually, she had become a knitter.

She was knitting little tiny sweaters
for her kitty cats.

That was SO amazing!

But not as amazing as when we went sailing.

We climbed aboard the boat and as soon as we set sail, we found out that the captain was really a—

He was a bloodthirsty pirate who was making
your granny walk the plank?
But you stole a sword, beat him
in a swashbuckling fight, took his treasure map,
and found the buried treasure?

Umm . . . no. No.
Actually, he was really a fifth grade science teacher!

He was on the boat to study seaweed!

That was SO amazing!

But not as amazing as when we went hiking up a mountain.

We were climbing up a rocky trail when
I slipped and crashed into a—

And he had locked your granny in a dungeon,
and he tried to perform dastardly experiments on you?
But you saved your granny and escaped just before
the whole place exploded?

Umm . . . no. No.
Actually, I crashed into
a blueberry bush.

I landed on a bunch of blueberries,
but they didn't even stain my shorts.

That was SO amazing!

But not as amazing as when we went
for a walk in the woods.

We walked into a small clearing and there, right in front of us, we saw a—

DINOSAUR?!?

A giant T. Rex stomped out of the woods
and chased you for miles? But just as it was about to grab you,
you jumped on top of it, wrestled it to the ground,
and saved your family?

Umm . . . no. No. Actually, we saw a cute little chipmunk.

I tossed a piece of my sandwich to him and he almost ate it!

That was SO amazing!

But none of that is as amazing as my new friend.

He really wants to meet all of you. He's SO amazing!

ALBERT!!
Nothing you did is amazing.
It's all boring, Albert.

Boring, boring, boring.

Lame.

Dull.

Humdrum.

Pathetic.

Really, really, really boring.

Sorry, Albert, but we're leaving.

Bye, Albert.

Later, dude.

So long.

See you, Albert.

Bye.

Hey, guys!
Come back!
My friend traveled a long way to get here.
He came all the way from . . .

OUTER SPACE!